# This book belongs to

_____

# WALT DISNEY

### VOLUME 7

# MICKEY
# FINDS A KITTEN

## WALT DISNEY FUN-TO-READ LIBRARY

## A BANTAM BOOK
### TORONTO ● NEW YORK ● LONDON ● SYDNEY ● AUCKLAND

Mickey Finds a Kitten   A Bantam Book/January 1986   All rights reserved.   Copyright © 1986 Walt Disney Productions.   This book may not be reproduced, in whole or in part, by mimeograph or any other means.

ISBN 0-553-05583-6

Published simultaneously in the United States and Canada.   Bantam Books are published by Bantam Books, Inc.   Its trademark, consisting of the words ''Bantam Books'' and the portrayal of a rooster, is Registered in U.S. Patent and Trademark Office and in other countries.   Marca Registrada.   Bantam Books, Inc., 666 Fifth Avenue, New York, New York 10103.   Printed in the United States of America   0 9 8 7 6 5 4 3 2 1

Mickey came home from his afternoon walk.
Pluto ran to him. He barked. *"Arf! Arf-arf!"*
That meant, "I'm glad you are back."

Mickey just said, "Hello, Pluto." He did
not pet him. Mickey looked at something that
was in the box he held. "You're okay now,
kitty," he said.

"*Meow*," said the something in the box.

Out popped a very small kitten.

"Hungry, kitty?" Mickey asked. He gave her a bowl of milk.

Pluto walked over to his water bowl. *"Arf!"* he barked. That meant, "Please fill my water bowl."

But Mickey didn't hear him.

Pluto picked up his bowl. But Mickey
didn't see him. He just kept petting the kitten.
"Stay out of the way of cars, kitty cat," he
said. "I'm glad I came along and saved you."

Mickey went into the living room, and the kitten ran after him.

Mickey laughed. "You are really something else!" he said. "Just look at the way you follow me!"

Pluto's ears stood up. Was following a special thing to do? He always followed Mickey.

The kitten played with Mickey's hat.
Mickey laughed again.

Pluto watched the kitten. Was playing
with Mickey's hat special too? He thought
about that for quite a while.

The kitten jumped up into Mickey's chair. Pluto watched and wondered. <u>He</u> couldn't sit in Mickey's chair. Not ever!

But Mickey didn't say one word to the kitten. He just smiled and sat in another chair.

That night Pluto slept on the floor beside
Mickey's bed.
The kitten slept right on Mickey's bed!

The next day, the kitten woke Mickey up
<u>very</u> early to say good morning!
But Mickey wasn't angry. Instead he just
laughed.

Pluto said good morning too.

But Mickey didn't laugh. He said, "Cut that out, Pluto. Remember you aren't a puppy anymore."

*Thump!* The morning paper came.

Pluto heard it, and he thought of a nice thing he could do. He ran and got the paper. He didn't make a hole in it. He didn't even drop it. He just put it on the floor at Mickey's feet.

"Thanks, Pluto," said Mickey. "You're a good dog." He patted Pluto's head.

Pluto felt good. There! Now Mickey knew what great things Pluto could do.

While Mickey went to dress, the kitten started to play. She jumped on the paper. She pulled it and she tore it. When Mickey came back, the paper was all in pieces.

"Now, why did you do that, kitty?" asked
Mickey. But he didn't scold her.
Pluto watched and wondered. *"Rowf!"* he
barked. *Rowf* meant, "I don't understand!"

Pluto went outside and lay down under a tree. He put his head on his paws, and he thought about things.

Soon Morty and Ferdie came along.
"Look at all those leaves," said Morty.
"Let's clean them up," said Ferdie.
Pluto watched them rake the leaves into
one big pile.

Then the kitten came outside. She
jumped into the leaves, and she rolled over
and over.

"Look at her!" said Ferdie.

"She sure is having fun," said Morty.

Pluto thought he would have some fun too. He jumped into the leaves. He rolled over and over. The leaves flew all around.

"*Arf-arf-arf!*" he barked. That meant, "This sure is fun!"

Did Morty and Ferdie laugh? Did they say, "Look at old Pluto having fun?"

No! They did not.

"Now we have to do all this work over again," said Ferdie.

"Go away, Pluto," said Morty.

Pluto went off by himself.
Nobody liked anything he did anymore.
But they liked everything the kitten did. Was it
better to be a kitten than a dog?

Then Pluto saw Minnie. He liked Minnie, and Minnie liked him.

"*Ruff-ruff-ruff!*" Pluto barked. That meant, "I'm happy to see you."

Minnie said, "Hi, Pluto. I don't have time for you right now. But where is that dear little kitten that Mickey told me so much about?

"Here, kitty, kitty! What a sweet little thing you are," she said. She patted the kitten.
The kitten purred.
"What a nice noise," said Minnie.

Pluto watched and listened. Then he made a
noise too. He thought it was a beautiful noise. But
he was the only one who thought so.

Lunchtime came. Mickey and Minnie and
Morty and Ferdie sat around the table.
But not Pluto. He sat on the floor.

The kitten jumped up onto Mickey's lap.
"Well, well," Mickey laughed. "Hello there,
kitty. Do you want something to drink?

"How would you like some nice, cold milk, kitty?" asked Mickey. He poured some milk into a bowl.
The kitten drank up all the milk.

Pluto watched. And he thought. Perhaps
it <u>was</u> better to be a kitten than a dog. Maybe
everyone would like him again if he acted
like a kitten.

So Pluto jumped up onto Mickey's lap.
Did Mickey say, "Well, well. Hello there,
Pluto"? He did not. He said, "Pluto, what has
gotten into you. This is no way for you to act
at lunchtime!"

Pluto left the table. He lay down in the corner.

The kitten sat with her paws on the table.

But Pluto wanted to be near everyone.
He wanted to show them what a good kitten
he could be. *"ROUF-rouf!"* he barked. That
meant, "See me be a kitten."

Pluto put his great big paws on the table. Dishes went this way. Glasses went that way. Minnie and Morty and Ferdie jumped up.

"Pluto, go into the other room!" ordered Mickey.

All Pluto had wanted was to drink some milk, just the way he had seen the kitten do.

Pluto crawled away while Mickey picked up things. Minnie helped put things away. Morty and Ferdie petted the kitten. They were all very angry at Pluto.

Pluto lay by the door. He felt bad . . . bad . . . bad. He could never be a kitten!

Mickey thought for a minute. Then he said, "I think I know what's going on. We have not been very nice to Pluto. He is trying to act like a kitten. Maybe he thinks being a dog is not good enough."

"But that isn't true," said Morty. "Pluto is a great <u>dog</u>. Remember when we were little, Pluto?"

"You were the best baby-sitter we ever had," said Ferdie.

"You are still the best watchdog," said Minnie. "I am never afraid when you are nearby."

"Pluto," Mickey said, "we are
best friends! Nobody can ever take your
place with me."
Pluto grinned. He wagged his tail.

"You are the world's best dog," said
Mickey. "And don't you ever forget it!"
*"Meow?"* asked the kitten. That meant,
"Can I grow up to be just like you, Pluto?"

"*Arf,*" barked Pluto. "*Arf-arf-arf.*" And that meant, "I'll never change. I give my word. I'm glad I am me, good old Pluto!"